Little Sweet Potato

By Amy Beth Bloom   Illustrated by Noah Z. Jones

KATHERINE TEGEN BOOKS
An Imprint of HarperCollins Publishers

Katherine Tegen Books is an imprint of HarperCollins Publishers.

Little Sweet Potato

Text copyright © 2012 by Amy Bloom

Illustrations copyright © 2012 by Noah Z. Jones

All rights reserved. Printed in the United States of America.

No part of this book may be used or reproduced in any manner whatsoever without written permission except in the case of brief quotations embodied in critical articles and reviews. For information address HarperCollins Children's Books, a division of HarperCollins Publishers, 10 East 53rd Street, New York, NY 10022.

www.harpercollinschildrens.com

Library of Congress Cataloging-in-Publication Data is available.

ISBN 978-0-06-180439-7

Typography by Rachel Zegar

12 13 14 15 16   LP   10 9 8 7 6 5 4 3 2 1

First Edition

This is for Izzy
and for the original sweet potatoes,
Caitlin and Sarah.
—A.B.

For my two tater tots Eli and Sylvie
and my favorite sweet potato, Diane.
—N.Z.J.

Once upon a time, there was a little sweet potato who lived in a garden patch, where the earth was rich and brown and the air smelled sweet and spicy. He had never been anywhere else at all.

Sweet Potatoes

Just as Little Sweet Potato was beginning to get a peek at the world around him, there was a terrible quaking and shaking, and everyone in the garden patch held on to their vines for dear life. Little Sweet Potato got shaken loose and landed—

PLOP—

in the middle of a new and not-so-nice place.

"Where am I?" he wondered. "And how do I get back home?
And how will I know home when I get there?"

There was no one to answer him.

Little Sweet Potato pulled together all of his sweet-potato courage
and went rolling over to a garden patch at the edge of the road.

"Excuse me," Little Sweet Potato said very politely. "Do I belong here?"

They looked at him. They looked at one another. They fluffed their leafy green tops and wiggled their long orange bodies.

"We think not," they said. "You are lumpy, dumpy, and—we have to say it—you're bumpy. You don't belong here."

Little Sweet Potato rolled away as quickly as he could. He didn't know the world had such mean vegetation in it.

Trying to be brave, Little Sweet Potato rolled off to another patch, hoping things would go a little better and be a little nicer. "Excuse me," said Little Sweet Potato. "I wonder . . . I mean, do you think there might be a place for me in this garden?"

They looked at him and they looked at one another.

"Well, lemme think," the biggest rumbled. "Nope. See, we are handsome and purple with skin like satin. And the fact is, you are dumpy, bumpy, and kinda lumpy. What I'm trying to say, pal, is—scram."

And Little Sweet Potato rolled away. He didn't know the world had such scary vegetation in it.

"I'm down but I'm not out," Little Sweet Potato said bravely. And even though his feelings were mashed very soft and tender from all the rough handling, he rolled himself to the edge of another garden.

"Excuse me," he said. "Do you think, maybe, I could move in next to you?"

"Oh my goodness!" They giggled. Their long green arms covered their velvety blue and yellow faces. "Oh, dear, we don't think so. You're not even a flower. You're a lumpy, bumpy, dumpy vegetable, and *we're* beautiful. No offense."

And they waved good-bye as Little Sweet Potato rolled off.

The rest of the day was just as bad.
Bunches of round fruit, shiny and bright as
green marbles, told him to get lost.

Pink and puffy and sweet-smelling flowers with soft petals and sharp stickers told him there was no room in their garden.

Curvy, green-striped vegetables with bent necks and beautiful yellow flowers told him to shove off.

"That's it," said Little Sweet Potato. "There's just no place for me."

I am all alone, he thought, and one big tear rolled down his dear bumpy-sweet-potato face.

"Who, me?" Little Sweet Potato didn't know he was being called. Was he a sweet potato? Was he Bumpalicious?

Little Sweet Potato did roll toward the voice, his little sweet-potato heart beating fast.

"Excuse me," he said when he got to the patch.

"What for? We're just so glad you found your way back home,"
a lumpy, dumpy, and wonderfully bumpy sweet potato said very kindly.

"Home?" said Little Sweet Potato.

He felt himself glowing as brightly as the sun.

"I'm home?"

"Absolutely!" said the big, bumpy, and magnificently lumpy sweet potato. "And in the world's greatest garden. With fruits and vegetables and some flowers so fancy even I don't know what they are."

"Some just like their own kind," one of the pansies said sweetly.
"But we're the kind that like *all* kinds."

"You're so nice," said Little Sweet Potato. "I met some flowers who looked just like you, but they *weren't* very nice."
"Some are, some aren't," said a friendly carrot. "We are."

"That's how it is, kid," said a gleaming eggplant.

"It's not all mulch and sunshine out there."

"Oh, I *know*," said Little Sweet Potato.

"All kinds," said the big sweet potato. "Teeny and tall, big and small, fat as a ball and skinny as a stick. Of course, I happen to think lumpy, dumpy, and bumpy is especially nice."

"Me too," said Little Sweet Potato.

At least, he thought he said it. He was getting awfully sleepy.

He rolled into the patch on a spot that seemed just the right size—Little Sweet Potato size. He nestled into the rich, brown earth and gazed at the sky, and the trees, and the vegetables, and the flowers, and he settled down with a smile on his sweet-potato face.

How wonderful to be a sweet potato. How wonderful to be home at last.